The BENCH

By

Meghan, The Duchess of Sussex

Pictures by Christian Robinson

tundra

Tundra Books, an imprint of Penguin Random House Canada Young Readers, a division of Penguin Random House of Canada Limited

Library and Archives Canada Cataloguing in Publication available upon request
ISBN 978-0-7352-7216-3 (hardcover) | ISBN 978-0-7352-7217-0 (EPUB)

The artist used acrylic paint, colored pencil, and a bit of digital manipulation to create the illustrations for this book.
The text of this book is set in 17-point Jazmin. Interior design by Martha Rago and Christian Robinson.

Published simultaneously in the United States by Random House Children's Books, a division of Penguin Random House LLC, New York

Printed in the United States of America

www.penguinrandomhouse.ca

1 2 3 4 5   25 24 23 22 21

Penguin
Random House
tundra | TUNDRA BOOKS

For the man and the boy
who make my heart go
pump-pump

This is your bench
Where life will begin
For you and our son
Our baby, our kin.

This is your bench
Where you'll witness great joy.

From here you will rest
See the growth of our boy.

He'll learn to ride a bike
As you watch on with pride.

He'll run and he'll fall
And he'll take it in stride.

You'll love him.
You'll listen.
You'll be his supporter.

When life feels in shambles

You'll help him find order.

You'll sit on this bench
As his giving tree.

Some days he may cry
Perched there on your knee.

He'll feel happiness, sorrow
One day be heartbroken.

You'll tell him "I love you"
Those words always spoken.

This is your bench
For papa and son . . .

To celebrate joys
And victories won.

And here in the window
I'll have tears of great joy . . .

Looking out at My Love
And our beautiful boy.

Right there on your bench
The place you'll call home . . .

With daddy and son . . .

Where you'll never be 'lone.